MAR 2013

W9-CYT-286

Dear Parents and Educators,

Welcome to Penguin Young Readers! As parents and educators, you know that each child develops at his or her own pace—in terms of speech, critical thinking, and, of course, reading. Penguin Young Readers recognizes this fact. As a result, each Penguin Young Readers book is assigned a traditional easy-to-read level (1–4) as well as a Guided Reading Level (A–P). Both of these systems will help you choose the right book for your child. Please refer to the back of each book for specific leveling information. Penguin Young Readers features esteemed authors and illustrators, stories about favorite characters, fascinating nonfiction, and more!

Cork & Fuzz: Best Friends

LEVEL **3**

GUIDED READING LEVEL **J**

This book is perfect for a **Transitional Reader** who:
- can read multisyllable and compound words;
- can read words with prefixes and suffixes;
- is able to identify story elements (beginning, middle, end, plot, setting, characters, problem, solution); and
- can understand different points of view.

Here are some **activities** you can do during and after reading this book:
- Compare/Contrast: Cork is a muskrat, and Fuzz is a possum. But by the end of the book, they become great friends. How are Cork and Fuzz different? How are they alike?
- Find all the words in the story that have an -ed ending. On a separate sheet of paper, write the root word next to each word with an -ed ending. The chart below will get you started:

word with an -ed ending	root word
looked	look
yelled	yell

Remember, sharing the love of reading with a child is the best gift you can give!

—Bonnie Bader, EdM
    Penguin Young Readers program

*Penguin Young Readers are leveled by independent reviewers applying the standards developed by Irene Fountas and Gay Su Pinnell in *Matching Books to Readers: Using Leveled Books in Guided Reading*, Heinemann, 1999.

For Tom, always #1—DC

To Kenny and Richard—LM

Penguin Young Readers
Published by the Penguin Group
Penguin Group (USA) Inc., 375 Hudson Street, New York, New York 10014, USA
Penguin Group (Canada), 90 Eglinton Avenue East, Suite 700, Toronto, Ontario M4P 2Y3, Canada
(a division of Pearson Penguin Canada Inc.)
Penguin Books Ltd., 80 Strand, London WC2R 0RL, England
Penguin Group Ireland, 25 St. Stephen's Green, Dublin 2, Ireland (a division of Penguin Books Ltd.)
Penguin Group (Australia), 250 Camberwell Road, Camberwell, Victoria 3124, Australia
(a division of Pearson Australia Group Pty. Ltd.)
Penguin Books India Pvt. Ltd., 11 Community Centre, Panchsheel Park, New Delhi—110 017, India
Penguin Group (NZ), 67 Apollo Drive, Rosedale, Auckland 0632, New Zealand
(a division of Pearson New Zealand Ltd.)
Penguin Books (South Africa) (Pty.) Ltd., 24 Sturdee Avenue,
Rosebank, Johannesburg 2196, South Africa

Penguin Books Ltd., Registered Offices: 80 Strand, London WC2R 0RL, England

All rights reserved. No part of this book may be reproduced, scanned, or distributed in any printed or
electronic form without permission. Please do not participate in or encourage piracy of copyrighted
materials in violation of the author's rights. Purchase only authorized editions.

Text copyright © 2005 by Dori Chaconas. Illustrations copyright © 2005 by Lisa McCue. All rights
reserved. First published in 2005 as *Cork & Fuzz* by Viking and in 2010 by Puffin Books, imprints of
Penguin Group (USA) Inc. Published in 2012 by Penguin Young Readers, an imprint of
Penguin Group (USA) Inc., 345 Hudson Street, New York, New York 10014. Manufactured in China.

The Library of Congress has cataloged the Viking edition
under the following Control Number: 2004013613

ISBN 978-0-14-241593-1   10 9 8 7 6 5 4 3 2 1

CORK&FUZZ

Best Friends

by Dori Chaconas
illustrated by Lisa McCue

Penguin Young Readers
An Imprint of Penguin Group (USA) Inc.

Chapter 1

Cork the muskrat looked behind a thorn bush.

"Nobody here," he said.

He looked behind a pine tree.

"Nobody there," he said.

He picked up a small stone.

He dropped it.

He let out a big sigh.

"Nobody anywhere," Cork said.

Cork found a hollow log.

"Nothing to do!" he yelled into the log.

"Nothing to do!" an echo called back.

"Boring!" Cork called.

"Boring!" the echo called back.

"I have to go home now," Cork called.

"Can I come with you?" the echo asked.

Cork jumped back.

He scratched his head.

"Well, okay," he said.

"I guess I can roll you there."

Cork pushed.

The log began to roll.

"Uh-oh!" cried the echo.

The log bumped down a hill.

"Ow!"

The log bumped over a rock.

"Ow! *Ow!*"

It bumped into a big thorn bush.

"Ee-yow!"

A fat possum fell out.

"You are not an echo!" Cork said.

"What were you doing in that log?"

"Rolling," the possum said.

"And snacking."

He held up a shiny, black beetle.

"Want a bite?" the possum asked.

"Uck," Cork said.

He covered his eyes.

"I do not like beetles!"

"What do you like?" the possum asked.

"I like cattails," Cork said.

"I like roots.

I like seeds."

"Uck!" the possum said.

"Veggie stuff!"

Then Cork did not hear anything more.

He opened his eyes.

The possum had disappeared.

Chapter 2

Cork heard a noise behind him.

The possum popped out of the bushes.

Then he put something under

a pointed leaf.

"What is that?" Cork asked.
"What did you put under that
pointed leaf?"
"Just a little nothing," the
possum said.

He stuck his nose against Cork's nose.

"My name is Fuzz," the possum said.

"My name is Cork," said Cork.

"Are you a duck?" Fuzz asked.

"Ducks go *cork! Cork!*"

"Ducks do not go *cork! Cork!*" Cork said.

"Ducks go *quack! Quack!*

I am a muskrat.

I float like a cork."

"Do you want to play something?"

Fuzz asked.

"We could play hide-and-seek," Cork said.

"Or we could play find-and-*eat*," Fuzz said.

"We find beetles.

Then we eat them."

"Uck," Cork said.

"We could play catch-the-pinecone,"

Cork said.

He picked up a stick.

He swung it at a pine tree branch.

A pinecone fell.

It landed on Fuzz's head. *Thunk!*

Fuzz gasped.

Then he fell to the ground.

He did not move.

He did not move at all.

Chapter 3

Fuzz lay very still on the ground.

Cork bent down and wiggled Fuzz's tail.

Fuzz did not move.

Cork wiggled Fuzz's nose.

He wiggled Fuzz's foot.

Fuzz did not move.

Cork sat on the ground next to Fuzz.

Cork sniffled.

"I will stay here with you," Cork said.

A butterfly landed on Fuzz's ear.

"Shoo!" Cork said.

A grasshopper landed on Fuzz's paw.

"Shoo!" Cork said.

A caterpillar crawled up on Fuzz's belly.

"Shoo!" Cork said.

"Please do not be fainted much longer," Cork said.

Fuzz's eyes popped open.

"I am not fainted," Fuzz said.

"I was playing possum."

"Possum is not a fun game to play," Cork said.

"It is not a game," Fuzz said.

"It is what possums do when they are afraid.

Something hit me on the head.

I was afraid."

"It was only a pinecone," Cork said.

"A pinecone?" Fuzz said.

"I thought it was a giant buzzard bee."

Fuzz pushed the pinecone with his toe.

Then he picked something up off
the ground.

He put it under the pointed leaf.

"What was that?" Cork asked.

"Just a little nothing," Fuzz answered.

Chapter 4

"I can teach you to play pin-the-tail-on-the-turtle," Cork said.

Cork found a long leaf.

He stuck a thorn in the end of the leaf.

"This is the turtle's tail," Cork told Fuzz.

"This is not a fun game for the turtle," Fuzz said.

"He has got a thorn in his tail!"

"No, no, no!" Cork said.

"This is a pretend tail!"

Cork gave the leaf to Fuzz.

"That stump is a pretend turtle."

"Close your eyes.

Now stick the tail on the turtle.

I will find a leaf for me."

Cork bent over to pick up a leaf.

"Ee-yow!" he yelled.

"Uh-oh," said Fuzz.

"I am not the turtle!" Cork said.

"Do not stick the tail on me!"

"I am sorry," Fuzz said.

He hung his head.

Then he picked something up off
the ground.

He put it under the pointed leaf.

Cork stuck his nose against Fuzz's nose.

"What are you hiding under that
pointed leaf?" Cork said.

"Okay, I will show you," Fuzz said.

"But you will think it is silly."

Fuzz picked up the pointed leaf.
Under the leaf were three stones:
a red stone, a white stone, and
a shiny, black stone.

"I collect interesting stones," Fuzz said.

At first Cork looked surprised.

Then he laughed.

"I knew you would laugh," Fuzz said.

"I will go home now."

"No, no, no!" Cork said.

"I am laughing because I collect

stones, too!

Come to my pond!

I will show you my stones."

"You live in a pond?" Fuzz asked.

"Yes," said Cork.

"Like a duck!" Fuzz said.

"Ducks live in ponds."

Cork picked up Fuzz's stones.

"Come on," said Cork, "and I will explain

again about muskrats and ducks."

"Cork, cork," quacked Fuzz.